AGENT Amelia Ghost Diamond!

AGENT Amelia

Ghost Diamond!

MICHAEL BROAD

Andersen Press
London

First published
in 2007 by
Andersen Press Limited,
20 Vauxhall Bridge Road,
London SW1V 2SA
www.andersenpress.co.uk

Printed and bound in Great Britain by
Cox & Wyman Ltd, Reading, Berkshire

Copyright
© Michael Broad, 2007
All rights reserved.
British Library Cataloguing in
Publication Data available.
ISBN 978 1 84270 662 6

For Shannon

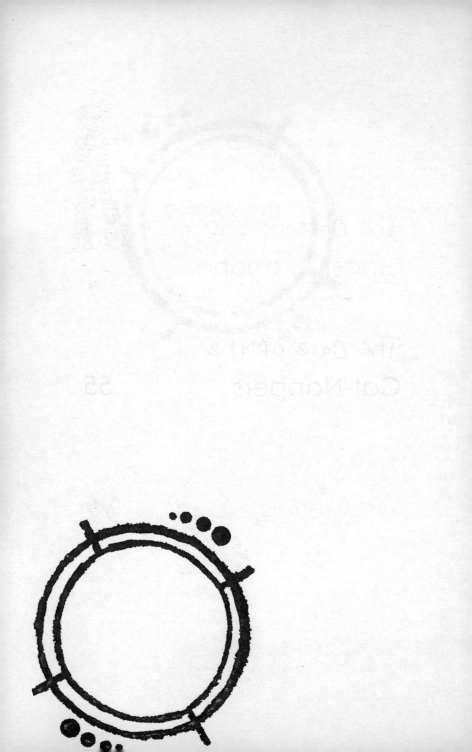

I'M AMELIA KIDD and I'm a secret agent.

Well, I'm not actually a secret agent. I don't work for the government or anything, but I've saved the world loads of times from evil geniuses and criminal masterminds. There are loads of them around if you know what to look for.

I'm really good at disguises. I make my own gadgets (which sometimes work), and I'm used to improvising in sticky situations — which you have to do all the time when you're a secret agent.

These are my Secret Agent Case Files.

 The Case of the Ghost Diamond

'What on earth do you have in that rucksack?' Mum said, leaning out of the car window as I heaved the bag off the back seat and onto my shoulders. It was pretty heavy but I tried to pretend it wasn't.

'Stuff,' I said, peering over my sunglasses to gauge her reaction.

'Stuff!'

Mum said, with a suspicious frown. And the way she said 'stuff' meant she wanted to know exactly what kind of 'stuff' and why I had so much of it.

'Just boring school trip stuff,' I smiled, and legged it for the school gates.

Being vague is the best thing to do when you're under interrogation. Mum would have to really want to know what was in my bag to come after me and continue the line of questioning, but I'd deliberately

dawdled back at the house so I knew
she was already running late.

You have to think ahead when
you're a secret agent.

'Well, have a nice time then,'

Mum called out, and then quickly
drove away.

Phew!

I couldn't tell Mum my bag was full of secret agent stuff or she'd think I'd gone bonkers. When you're a secret agent you can't tell anyone or else they'd worry when you're off saving the world all the time.

Especially my mum, who gets her knickers in a twist whenever I go to the shops on my own!

My class were
already boarding
the bus to take us
to the museum,
so I stayed at the

back and watched our teacher, Mrs
Granger, ticking everyone off her list.

Mrs Granger had been under
my surveillance for a week and I
was pretty sure she was a criminal
mastermind posing as a teacher. I was
also pretty sure something dodgy was
about to go down at the museum.

Mrs Granger had planned the museum trip so our class could see a famous treasure called the Ghost Diamond, a pendant containing the biggest diamond in the world. Usually school trips are educational, but the Ghost Diamond had nothing to do with our school work so it didn't make sense. Then I snooped around the school library records and discovered Mrs Granger

had recently checked out two very suspicious-sounding books.

One was called *Hypnotism for Beginners* and the other was called *Ancient Jewels and Curses*.

The second one was a very strange subject for a book and bit too much of a coincidence if you ask me!

My teacher was definitely up

to something and I had to get to the bottom of it.

When it was my turn to board the bus Mrs Granger blocked my way with her clipboard.

'Amelia Kidd, will you please take off those ridiculous sunglasses!' she shrieked, and she shrieked it loud enough for the whole bus to hear, so everyone started giggling.

If Mrs Granger suspected me of
being a secret agent then she'd just
done a very good job of drawing
attention away from herself
and onto me, which is
definitely the sort
of thing an evil
genius might
do.
I took
off my
sunglasses
and Mrs
Granger
prodded my rucksack with her
clipboard.

'And what do you have in the
bag?' she said. 'The kitchen sink?'

The whole bus
giggled again, but
I didn't lose my
cool.
'My packed
lunch and my
big winter coat,'
I lied. Well, I did
have my packed
lunch, but not my winter coat. 'Mum
said I have to take a coat because it
might turn chilly.'

If a teacher starts
questioning you,
I've found it's a very
good idea to blame
everything on
your mum, then
they can't say
anything about
it and they would
never bother to phone up and check.

'Sunglasses *and* a winter coat,'
Mrs Granger said, waving me onto
the bus with an exhausted sigh.
'Amelia Kidd, you really have come
prepared!'

The other kids giggled again as
I made my way down the aisle to the
back of the bus, but under my breath
I said, 'Yes, Mrs Granger, I've come

prepared.' And slipped my sunglasses back on. Inside the museum I was keeping a close eye on Mrs Granger when I noticed she'd switched her shoes! She was wearing bright pink trainers that looked very new and very odd because the rest of her clothes were all dark and old-fashioned.

I'd never seen Mrs Granger wearing trainers before. She always wore sensible black shoes. This was

another clue pointing
to something big
going down at the
museum, but I
had to keep alert
and not let my
teacher know I
was onto her,
or she might
postpone her
criminal activity
for another day.

'I like your trainers, Mrs Granger,' said Trudy Hart, who is always sneaking around the teachers. I don't like Trudy Hart. She's very popular in school and is always mean to people who aren't, like me.

'Why, thank you, Trudy,' said Mrs Granger. 'They're new.'

'They look very pretty on you,' Trudy added with a slimy smile.

'Do you think so?' Mrs Granger smiled, turning her heel to admire the new trainers. 'Of course, field trips involve an awful lot of walking, so I'm wearing them mostly for comfort.'

'Or to make a quick getaway, more like!' I whispered.

Mrs Granger's head snapped up and she narrowed her eyes at me.

Uh Oh!

Mrs Granger told us to explore

the museum on our own and gave
instructions to meet back at the gift
shop in an hour. After my comment
about the shoes I knew she'd be
keeping an eye on me, but I needed
to keep an eye
on her.

I went
straight to the

ladies' loo and propped a bin against
the door so I wouldn't be disturbed.
Then, in front of the mirror, I

rummaged inside my rucksack and produced a large flowery dress and a plum-coloured wig.

Pulling the dress on over my school uniform, I tucked my hair inside the wig and adjusted everything in the mirror. Once satisfied that I didn't look like me anymore, I slipped my sunglasses back on and headed for the door.

BANG! BANG! BANG!

Someone was on the other side of the door trying to get in!

'Amelia Kidd!' said a loud angry voice. 'I demand you let me in this instant!'

It was Trudy Hart! And by the sound of giggling I guessed she had a couple of her equally mean cronies with her. She must have seen me come in and with a quick glance at the barred windows I realised I was completely trapped in the loo!

'My needs are greater than yours because I'm popular!' Trudy squealed and booted the door.

I checked

my disguise in the mirror again and wondered whether it would stand up to close scrutiny. Sometimes being a secret agent is all about thinking on your feet and taking chances, so I pulled my shoulders back, grabbed my bag and flung the door open.

'Well it's about time . . .' Trudy growled, and then stopped when she saw me.

'What a rude little girl!' I shrieked, in my best impression of a grown-up voice. I eyed Trudy up and down and prodded her with an authoritative finger. 'I have a very good mind to find your teacher!'

Trudy's mouth fell open and
her cronies gawped at me with wide
eyes.

Before any of
them could get a closer
look I stormed past
like an outraged
adult. They didn't say
anything or
come after me,
so I think they were
definitely
fooled. Which
was good because
I really did have
to find the teacher
and work out what she was up to.

I wondered if Mrs Granger
planned to steal the Ghost
Diamond? And if so, why? Criminal
masterminds and evil geniuses
are only ever interested in world

domination, so what could she want with a silly old pendant?

When I found Mrs Granger she was leaving the gift shop with a small brown bag. This was very suspicious because she'd told everyone to meet there in an hour. Also, nobody goes to the gift shop first, everyone goes afterwards to buy souvenirs, and you

can't buy a
souvenir of
somewhere
you haven't
properly
visited yet.

I hid
behind a
pillar until
Mrs Granger
passed me,
then I followed
at a safe distance, ducking
and diving and blending into the
crowd. As I suspected she was
heading for the room with the Ghost
Diamond, and she was looking
around her to make sure no one was
following.

Luckily, I'm used to tracking suspects so she didn't spot me.

In the Ghost Diamond room I made two holes in a guidebook and lurked close behind Mrs Granger, watching her carefully as she studied the jewel. After a couple of minutes she struck up a conversation with the security guard whose job it was to protect the pendant.

'. . . and why is it called the Ghost Diamond?' asked Mrs Granger casually.

Something told me she already knew and was just killing time, or trying to distract the security guard.

But he was standing right next to the jewel case so she couldn't do anything without him seeing.

The security guard explained that the white centre of the stone was believed to be the ghost of a very powerful spirit, a spirit who vowed to rule the world with whoever released him from his diamond prison.

Ding! Ding! Ding!
(That's the sound of alarm bells ringing in my head.)

My instinct was right, Mrs Granger did want to rule the world and now she was inches away from a dodgy diamond that would let her do exactly that!

While I was working all this out I noticed that Mrs Granger had opened the brown bag from the gift shop and was fiddling with something in her hands. But from where I stood I couldn't actually see what she was doing.

Not wanting to risk getting closer I rummaged inside my rucksack and pulled out my mirror-on-a-stick gadget, which sounds like an odd piece of secret agent equipment, but has got me out of a lot of scrapes in the past.

doing!

I positioned the mirror so I could get a close look at Mrs Granger's hands and saw that she had an exact copy of the Ghost Diamond pendant! Mrs Granger must have picked it up in the gift shop, and now she was swinging it from side to side in a very peculiar way.

I was so busy watching my
teacher I hadn't noticed the security
guard, who by this time had stopped
talking and was staring at the fake
pendant with a very glazed look in
his eyes.

Hypnotism for Beginners! I gasped.
Mrs Granger turned around
and gave me an angry glare, then she
sprang into action. With the security
guard too hypnotised to notice, she

smashed the lid of the jewel case with
her elbow, swapped the pendants
over and then scarpered in her new
pink trainers.

Shoving the
mirror back

in my rucksack
I legged it after
her, although
the big dress
was weighing
me down a bit
and it was kind
of difficult to see
through the long
plum fringe of my
wig.

Mrs
Granger
was getting
away!

Up ahead I noticed Trudy Hart standing by the gift shop with her cronies. She was my only chance to stop Mrs Granger getting away with the Ghost Diamond and taking over the world.

'Stop her!' I yelled at the top of my voice.

But Trudy just sneered and turned her nose up. I'm not sure whether she knew it was me, or just didn't want to help the angry grown-up who had prodded her with an authoritative finger, but it was obvious she didn't intend to stop the sprinting teacher.

As Mrs Granger neared the exit I had to think fast.

Pulling the rucksack off my shoulders, I swung it over my head to get up some speed and then lobbed it as hard as I could.

The bag sailed

through

the air . . .

. . . . and hit the floor at the teacher's
feet, the straps tangling around her
new pink trainers.

Mrs Granger was running
one minute and the next she was
sprawled out on the floor, but
she continued to slide along
the shiny marble like a
person-shaped bowling-ball
heading straight for Trudy
Hart and her cronies.
The girls watched in
horror, frozen to the
spot like tenpins in
a bowling alley
about to be
toppled.

CRASH!

Skidding to a halt
I snatched my rucksack
from the heap of groaning
people and slipped away
just in time.

All the non-hypnotised security guards suddenly swooped on Mrs Granger and because they weren't sure exactly what had happened, they pounced on Trudy Hart and her cronies too.

When you're a secret agent you can't ever take credit for saving the world, or else everyone would know who you are and you wouldn't be secret anymore. So by the time I got back from the ladies' loo, in my normal

clothes and with my normal hair,
Mrs Granger was being carted off by
the police.

All the kids in my class were
waiting on the steps of the museum,
so I wandered cautiously over to
Trudy Hart and her cronies who
were all looking a bit confused.

'What happened?' I said, with as much surprise on my face as I could fake.

One of Trudy's cronies burst into tears and Trudy rolled her eyes.

'Some mad woman attacked Mrs Granger,' she said, matter-of-factly.

'Oh,' I said. 'Then why are they taking Mrs Granger away?'

Trudy scratched her head.

'I think maybe she stole something from the gift shop?' she said, although it was obviously just a guess. 'I saw the security guards fighting her for a necklace or something; she seemed very angry.'

'Oh,' I said.

'The school has called our parents to come and collect us . . . ' Trudy added, and then stopped and frowned at me. She lifted a hand up to my hair and pulled out a long plum hair!

Uh Oh!

I snatched it back and let a swift breeze carry it from my fingers.

Trudy narrowed her eyes at me and was about to say something when I heard the sound of a familiar car horn. I looked out to the road and saw Mum winding the window

down and waving.

'Gotta go!' I said, and legged it before she could draw any conclusions.

I shoved my rucksack onto the back seat of the car and climbed in after it. Looking up at the museum steps I could see Trudy Hart was still frowning as if trying to work out if any of what she suspected was even possible.

'I'm sorry your trip was cut short,' Mum said, eyeing me through the rear-view mirror as we drove away. 'You can't have had time to see anything interesting at all?'

'I guess not,' I said, tipping my glasses and peering over the top.

'And you lugged that big bag around for nothing,' Mum added sadly.

I thought about it for a moment
and then smiled to myself.

'Oh, I wouldn't say that,' I said,
patting my faithful old rucksack.

The Case of the Cat-Nappers

'Amelia!' Mum yelled. 'What on earth do you think you're doing?'

'Bird watching,' I lied, without taking my eyes off the target.

'The point of binoculars is so you can see them from the ground.' Mum sighed. 'You really don't need to be halfway up a tree, now come down this instant before you snag your jumper!'

'OK,' I said. 'Just one more minute, I'm watching a very interesting bird.'

I wasn't really watching a bird – I was watching the trap I'd set earlier.

Cats had been mysteriously vanishing down my street. It began with one, which wasn't too suspicious because cats wander off all the time. But then another one disappeared, followed by another, and within a week there were no cats left at all!

I was pretty sure a criminal mastermind was planning to take over the world using stolen cats. They're always doing dodgy stuff like that. So I put my stuffed toy Tiddles out on the pavement as bait and waited for the cat-napper to nab it.

Mum continued to moan in the background when a white van suddenly turned the corner into our street.

I watched as it slowed to a crawl outside our house and quick as a flash the back doors flew open,

an arm snatched Tiddles and the van screeched away!

Adjusting the focus on my binoculars, I scanned the speeding vehicle and saw the words 'Smith's Fish' in blue lettering along the side.

The van belonged to the fish

shop around
the corner!
'Aha!' I
said, because
at last I
finally
had a
lead.
'Aha?'
Mum
inquired, as I
clambered down the branches.

'Oh, I was watching an Aha
Bird building a nest,' I said. 'They're
very rare.'

Mum frowned at my jumper and brushed pieces of bark and twigs away with her hand.

'I can't imagine why Gran agreed to knit you a black one,' Mum sighed. 'It really is the worst colour for showing up bits. And besides, black isn't very cheery for a girl of your age.'

'I like it,' I shrugged.

Of course my real reason for choosing black was that it would come

in handy during night-time manoeuvres. Also, when you're on surveillance up a tree in the daytime,

a bright pink jumper would be a dead giveaway. You have to think ahead when you're a secret agent.

Mum was heading back to the house when I suddenly had an idea.

'Can we have fish for dinner tonight?' I asked, tagging along behind.

'But you don't like fish,' she said. 'The last time we had fish you were ill.'

'That was when I was little,' I said. 'I'm pretty sure I like it now.'

'Hmmm, well, if you're sure,' Mum

said uncertainly. 'But you'll have to pop to the fish shop for me. I'm not going out again just because you've decided you like fish all-of-a-sudden.'

'OK,' I said casually, and slipped on my sunglasses.

On the way to Smith's Fish I discreetly collected 'LOST CAT'

posters from all the trees and
lampposts. Now I knew who'd
swiped the missing moggies I'd need
a list of telephone numbers to return
them.

Outside the fish shop I tucked
the posters into my rucksack and
rummaged around for an appropriate
disguise, although Mum's mention of

Gran had already given me an idea.

I pulled on an old plastic mac, crammed a short curly wig on my head and tied a see-through plastic rain hood on top of it. It wasn't raining – but old ladies

often wear rain hoods when it's not
raining.

A bell rang over my head,
wig and rain hood as I tottered into
Smith's Fish.

A short plump man hurried out
from the back of the shop and glared
at me. I guessed this was Mr Smith.
He stood over the counter, folded his
arms and sighed (as though he had

better things to do than serve old ladies – things like pinching people's pets!).

'What do you want?' he demanded.

'I'd like some fish, please,' I croaked, hunched over and gazing at the counter.

There wasn't a lot of fish to

choose from, just a couple of prawns and a crab. I guessed all the stock had been used up keeping the stolen cats happy – and not very successfully judging by the scratches on Mr Smith's hands.

'What kind of fish do you want?' he asked impatiently.

'Two nice pieces of haddock, please,' I said, peering over my sunglasses.

'We're all out
of haddock,'
he snapped.
'It's either
prawns,
crab or
nothing.'
'Oh,
well in that
case I'll just
have two nice pieces of haddock,
please,' I croaked, and while Mr
Smith was busy getting irritated I
surveyed the shop for any signs of
cats. The great thing about the old-
lady disguise is you
can keep people
distracted

for ages while you carry out basic surveillance.

'ARE YOU DEAF?' he yelled. 'I SAID WE'RE ALL OUT OF HADDOCK!'

'Yes, haddock,' I said. 'Two nice pieces, please.'

This went on for a while and Mr Smith was getting very red in the face, when a short plump woman suddenly appeared behind him. I figured this must be Mrs Smith, and she didn't look very happy either.

'What's going on out here?'
she growled, glaring sideways at her
husband.

'This deaf old bag wants
HADDOCK!' he growled back.

Mrs Smith
offered me an
unconvincing
smile.

'Then fetch
some from out the back!' she snarled.

'But . . . ' said Mr Smith.

'The job's going down tonight,
so we won't need it anymore,' hissed
Mrs Smith, through gritted teeth.

'And you're drawing

too much attention by standing here shouting about HADDOCK!'

The other great thing about the old-lady disguise is that people always think you're deaf – they whisper things thinking you can't hear them and always give vital details away.

Mrs Smith gave me another fake smile, grabbed her husband by the elbow and marched him out to the back of the shop, where they started arguing. I couldn't hear exactly what was said, but things like,

'Keep a low profile!'
and, 'Get rid of her!'
filtered into the shop.
The reason
I couldn't hear
them
properly
was
because
I'd leapt
over

the counter and was busy
rummaging through a pile
of papers beside the till – I
was looking for clues to
the exact location of the
cats.

Among the bills
and receipts I found a

strange map-like diagram!

I didn't have time to look properly, but I did see the word 'cat' among the various scribbles. Deciding the map must lead to the cats I shoved it in my plastic mac and crept back around the counter.

Mr Smith suddenly reappeared with a parcel wrapped in white paper.

'Two nice pieces of haddock, madam,' he said politely.

I didn't get a chance to study the map before dinner, so that evening I pretended to have an upset tummy and asked to go to bed early.

'I knew I shouldn't have let you have fish,' Mum sighed.

I shrugged my shoulders helplessly and shuffled off to my room.

Closing my bedroom door carefully I ran to the desk, flicked on the lamp and unfolded the piece of paper. On closer inspection I discovered it wasn't a map at all, it was a blueprint.

A blueprint of the local bank!

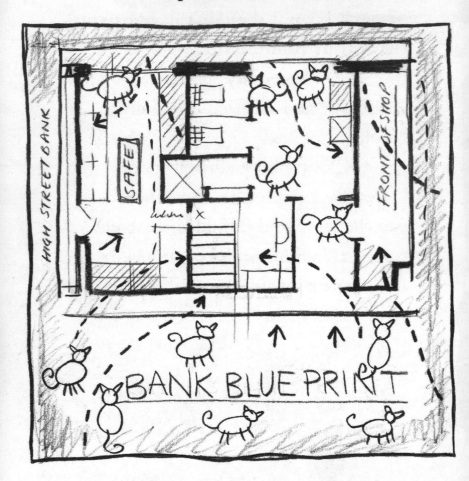

There was a diagram etched
over the blueprint with drawings

of cats and arrows pointing in and
out of the bank. I couldn't work
out exactly how, but it was clear
the Smiths had stolen the cats to
somehow pull off a bank robbery!

It surprised me that Mr and
Mrs Smith were only robbing a bank
and not planning to take over the
world. Everything about them said
criminal mastermind to me. Then
I turned the paper over and found a
note scribbled in the corner.

'After robbery — steal
more cats and then
TAKE OVER THE
WORLD!'

I knew it!

I also knew from
Mrs Smith's careless

whispering that the job was going down tonight – which didn't leave much time. So I stuffed my rucksack full of gadgets, dressed in black leggings, black jumper and a black woolly hat, and then shimmied down the drainpipe and headed straight for the high street.

I got to the bank just as Mr and Mrs Smith pulled up in their van.

Diving into
a nearby
doorway I
watched
from the
shadows
as Mrs
Smith tiptoed around the back of the
vehicle, flung the rear doors open
and clapped her hands
together twice.
Suddenly
dozens of
cats spilled
from the
van and
gathered
around
her feet.

Mrs Smith pulled a piece of fish from her pocket and whistled through her fingers. All of the cats immediately sat bolt upright and gazed at her intently; then she

whistled again and they formed an orderly line outside the bank.

The cats had all been trained!

I watched in amazement as the woman crouched down and began whistling a series of complicated commands. Each pair of furry ears

twitched in turn as she gave the
cats their instructions and a small
piece of fish. Then she stood up
and pointed to the bank.
Suddenly all the cats
sprang into action. Some
scaled the drainpipe, others
climbed up to the first floor
windows and a couple of the
smaller ones clambered through
the bank's deposit
box. Each cat found its
own way inside the bank
until there
were none
left on the
pavement
beside Mrs
Smith.

Mr Smith stayed in the van the whole time revving the engine, meaning he was obviously the getaway driver. But that also meant that once the cats returned the Smiths would speed away with all the cats and the loot!

I decided there was no way to stop the van without getting squashed, so I had to somehow prevent the animals from returning to the van. And I had to think fast because the first of the cat-burglars had already returned – followed by another, then another . . .

Some of the cats had wads of

money in their
mouths, others
were holding
bags of cash.
A few were
even wearing
diamond tiaras

and matching
necklaces
(and looking very pleased with
themselves)!

Mrs Smith stood among them and seemed to be counting heads.

I rummaged frantically in my rucksack for a gadget that might help me out, something to cause a big diversion or lure the cats away, but there was nothing appropriate.

Then I glanced down at my jumper . . .

Quick as a flash I snagged a thread, pulled a long length of wool from my sleeve and leapt from my hiding place.

'Here, puss-puss!' I shrieked.

Waving my arm in the air I
legged it past a startled Mrs Smith
and through the sea of newly wealthy

cats, twitching and dangling the thread over their bobbing heads.

As I'd hoped they started leaping up, wide-eyed and swiping at the wool with their paws.

I definitely had their attention, so before Mrs Smith could work out what was happening I scarpered down the high street trailing the wool behind me. The cats immediately gave chase – leaving

Mrs Smith alone outside the bank
with her mouth hanging open.

Mr Smith honked the horn and
his wife jumped back into the van,
and with a sudden shrieking of tyres
they chased me – and the trail of rich
moggies – down the high street.

Mr Smith was waving his fist in
the air and Mrs Smith was dangling
out of the window clapping and
whistling frantically. Luckily the cats

were more interested in the wool and
completely ignored them – but the
van was quickly gaining.

I turned into the nearest
alleyway and heard the van screech
to a halt behind me. Mr and Mrs
Smith leapt out and took up the
chase on foot. Glancing back I saw

they were now very red-faced,
although I wasn't sure if it was anger
or because they were both short and
plump and not used to running.

I had to think fast!

With no time to access my
rucksack I looked down at my
jumper again.

The thread from my right
sleeve was still trailing behind me so
I set to work unpicking the
left one, pulling out great
long loops of wool
one after the other,
and by the time I
reached the street I
had a big armful
of tangled
yarn.

I turned the corner and crouched behind the wall.

The cats gathered around my feet tapping the limp thread half-heartedly, when suddenly the panting couple staggered out of the alleyway. I immediately sprang up and threw the great loopy mess of wool over their heads like a big black web.

With the excitement of so much dangling wool the cats went mad again and started jumping all over the place swiping at anything that moved, and they mostly swiped at Mr and Mrs Smith who were trying to snatch the cash.

'Ow!' said Mr Smith.

'Moaw!' said the cats.

'Ow!' said Mrs Smith.

'Moaw!' said the cats.

In
all the
confusion I
circled the fishy
couple as fast as
I could,
winding wool
around their arms
and legs like a
spider wrapping a fly,
and the more their greedy hands
grabbed for the loot, the more
entangled they became.

Eventually I ran out of
wool and there was
nothing left of my
black jumper,
but by this
time

the cat–nappers were just a big black
blob, and so knotted up they couldn't
move an inch.

The cats were still swiping at loose threads dangling from the woolly cocoon when I noticed passers-by were stopping to watch the spectacle – which must have seemed very peculiar.

When you're a secret agent you can't take credit for saving the world all the time, or else you won't be secret anymore. So I pulled my woolly hat down over my face while I worked out what to do next.

Police sirens wailed in the distance, but I couldn't stick around to explain what had happened.

I had to think fast.

Squinting through

the woolly mesh of my hat I rummaged inside my rucksack again, desperately looking for a gadget that might get me out of another sticky situation.

Instead I laid my hands on the 'LOST CAT' posters and the bank blueprint!

'Aha!' I said, and I didn't mean a non-existent Aha Bird!

I pulled a loose thread from the top of the cocoon and attached the blueprint firmly to the heads of Mr and Mrs Smith. Then I stuck all the 'LOST CAT' posters around the woolly bundle – the police would definitely need to know who to phone once they'd de-cashed the millionaire moggies.

Nodding happily to myself at a case well solved, I pulled on my rucksack and disappeared into the night (in true secret agent style), although I did bump into a few people on the way because I couldn't really see where I was going.

I managed to sneak back into my room without Mum knowing,

but the next day I got into trouble for 'losing' my black jumper. Although Mum didn't make a big deal about it – I think she was secretly pleased.

In fact Mum was so not-annoyed that she rushed out and bought a bundle of bright pink wool. Then Gran set to work knitting me a brand new jumper, a proper cheery one for a girl of my age that wouldn't show up the bits.

Which is OK, because I like pink . . . when I'm not busy being a secret agent.

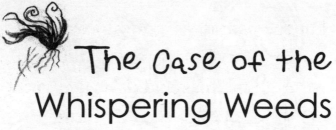

The Case of the Whispering Weeds

'Must you carry that big rucksack everywhere you go, Amelia?' Mum sighed, as I climbed into the back seat of the car. 'I really can't imagine what you think you need, we're only popping to the garden centre to fetch plant-food for my droopy roses.'

'Just dolls,' I lied, peering over my sunglasses.

Mum rolled her eyes as we drove away and started giving me a lecture about how I was too old to be

playing with dolls, and that perhaps I should make some real friends.

My rucksack was actually full of secret agent equipment, but I couldn't tell Mum or she'd worry about me. Saving the world can be dangerous and Mum was definitely better off thinking I was playing with dolls.

I was on a secret
mission to investigate
suspicious activity
going on at the
garden centre.
Sightings
of strange
creatures
– stuff
like that.
But it was too far away for me to
cycle, so every night after school I
crept into the garden to harass Mum's
favourite rose bushes. I'm not proud
of it, and I didn't do any real damage,
I just had to make sure they looked a
bit sad and droopy by the weekend.

You have to think ahead when
you're a secret agent.

I thought I was prepared for
anything when we reached the
garden centre, but I hadn't expected
to run into Trudy Hart! Trudy is in
my class and we don't get on at all.

'Isn't that your friend?' Mum
asked, when she spotted Trudy
wandering through the leafy aisles
with her dad. Mum must have seen

Trudy and me arguing at the school gates or something and wrongly assumed we were friends. 'No,' I said flatly, 'She's really not.'

'Yoo hoo!' Mum shrieked, grabbing my arm and pulling me over to where Trudy and her dad were arguing over bedding plants. It sounded like Trudy wanted only pink flowers in the garden and was giving him a really hard time about it.

Trudy and I glared at each other while our parents decided we two should go off together to look at flowers, and all meet up at the check out in an hour. Mum was clearly delighted that I'd be spending time with a real person instead of a doll, while Trudy's dad seemed only too pleased to dump her on me.

Parents always think that just because another kid is roughly the same age, you should have no problems being best friends with them. They don't even think about whether you have anything in common or not. Trudy and I have nothing in common. She's really popular at school and I don't have time to be popular because I'm too busy saving the world all the time.

"Bye, then,' I said to Trudy, as soon as we were out of sight of our parents.

'Yeah, good riddance!' snapped Trudy.

Reaching the end of the aisle, Trudy went one way and I went the other.

I had an investigation to carry out, but I couldn't risk Mum and Trudy seeing me in secret agent mode – or interfering while I'm trying to save the world. So I hid behind a large potted fern and I rummaged inside my rucksack.

I pulled on a big yellow summer dress over my clothes, scraped my hair into a frizzy blonde

wig and then crammed
a big floppy sunhat on
top. I could hardly see
through the frizzy
fringe and the
rim of the hat
and hoped that
meant no one
would recognise
me.

Turning the corner, my disguise
was immediately put to the test as I
ran straight into Mum!

'Why, I have that exact same
dress!' Mum said, conversationally.

It's no wonder
she recognised
it, it was
Mum's dress!

But I couldn't stand and have a conversation about it or Mum might also recognise her floppy sunhat and realise it was me.

'This old rag?' I shrieked, in my best impression of a posh woman's voice. 'It's hideous, I only ever use it for gardening!' And with that I grabbed the nearest pot plant and barged past Mum like I was the rudest

woman in the world.

'Well, really!' Mum exclaimed, shaking her head angrily.

I quickly plonked the plant into a nearby trolley and whizzed off to the opposite end of the garden centre. There I set to work looking for clues, filling the trolley as I went along like a real shopper would do.

You have to blend in when you're carrying out surveillance – it looks odd if you're just sneaking around.

I also kept an eye out for Mum and Trudy!

After half an hour of searching
I still hadn't found anything
suspicious in the garden centre, and
with only the greenhouse section left
I was beginning to think nothing
dodgy was going on after all.

I made my way slowly through
the aisles of greenhouses, feeling
bad about making Mum's roses
droopy for nothing, when something
suddenly shot across my path!

I froze to the spot, tipped my
sunglasses and scanned the floor.
I hadn't seen exactly what it was
because it moved too fast, but it was
bigger than a mouse and scuttled in
a very strange way like a small dark
octopus!

Crouching down
I noticed a faint
line of soil on
the white-tiled
floor!

Whatever
it was, the

creature had left a trail!

I immediately turned my trolley and set off after it and I was so busy watching

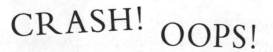

the trail of soil that I didn't notice when a man leapt out in front of my trolley! I dug my heels into the floor and rubber shrieked on tiles — but it was too late.

CRASH! OOPS!

'Look where you're going, you
silly old fool!' the man growled,
picking himself up from the floor
and patting the dust from his garden
centre uniform.
He was tall
and thin and
very mean-
looking.
   The man
obviously mistook
me for an old lady,

probably because I was hunched over and staring at the floor. So I went along with it and kept my face well hidden beneath the hat.

'Oh! Dearie me!' I croaked. 'I'm terribly sorry, young man.'

'And so you should be!' He snapped. 'There are some very rare plants in this section!' The man shook his fist angrily and then stormed away mumbling under his breath.

I decided it was very strange that the man had been so rude. People who work in shops are supposed to be nice to the customers, even if they mow you down with their trolley. Stranger still was his comment about rare plants. There didn't seem to be any plants at all in this section, just aisles of empty greenhouses.

Hmmm?

I kept an eye out for the strange man and picked up the trail of soil.

Before long the trail stopped dead outside one of the greenhouses. This greenhouse was right at the back of the showroom and was different from the rest. Not only was it bigger and older, but it was also clouded over with condensation so nothing could be seen through the hazy panes of glass.

Leaving the trolley in the aisle, I pushed the glass

door open a fraction and peered inside. The greenhouse was hot and humid and full of plants. But they weren't rare plants – or even common plants. All the plants in the misty greenhouse looked just like weeds!

I stepped inside and glanced around.

None of the plants were in pots or bedding trays, so they were definitely weeds. And they were scattered all over the floor as if someone had just weeded out their garden and dumped them there.

Hmmm?

Reaching inside my rucksack, I pulled out my extendable grabber-hand gadget (which is basically a hand on a stick). Whatever had scuttled across my path must be hiding under the weeds and I didn't want to use my real hand just in case the mysterious creature had teeth!

After a few minutes of careful poking I found nothing among the weeds, but I had to stop to catch my breath. The greenhouse was as hot as an oven and I was baking under the dress, hat and wig.

Realising no one could actually see me through the misted glass of the greenhouse, I peeled off my damp disguise and packed it away. But when I crouched down to refasten my rucksack I

suddenly heard a
strange sound
coming from
the weeds.

To
begin with, it
sounded like
the kind of
hissing that
grass makes
when it's
blown by
the breeze,
but listening
carefully it
began to
sound
more
and

more like whispering
– as though the weeds
were somehow talking
to each other!

It was then that
I realised something
dreadful.

The creature I'd been
tracking wasn't under the
weeds, the creature was
the weeds. And I was
trapped in a greenhouse

with a great big pile of them!

Uh Oh!

The weeds stopped whispering and slowly began to move, roots and leaves gathering around my feet, and some of the more stringy ones were trying to wrap their vines around my shoes!

I jumped back with a gasp.

The weeds immediately started whispering again and spread out in the floor of the greenhouse like a regiment of soldiers. Suddenly they leapt up onto their roots like little

white legs and scuttled after me
waving their leaves angrily in the air.

'ARRRRRGGGGHHH!' I
screamed, which admittedly isn't the
sort of thing you're supposed to do
when you're a secret agent, but they

were really creepy and they took me
by surprise.

I threw the door open and was
about to scarper when I saw a tall,
thin figure blocking my path! It was
the man I'd knocked over with my
trolley, and he was smiling at me.

But it wasn't a
friendly smile – it was
an I'm-going-to-rule-
the-world smile. I've
seen it loads of times
before, criminal
masterminds and
evil geniuses
always have an
I'm-going-to-
rule-the-world smile.

'So you found my
rare plants?' he
chuckled.
I glanced
behind me
at the weeds.
They were
still standing

on their roots but they'd stopped scuttling. They seemed to be looking up at the man as if waiting for his instructions.

The best thing to do when confronted by a criminal mastermind or an evil genius is to keep cool and not let them know you're scared. It was difficult, especially knowing the

whispering weeds were right behind me, but I gave the man my best fearless glare.

'You won't get away with this!'
I growled, and waved my extendable
grabber-hand at him.

'Won't get away with what?'
asked the man, frowning at my
gadget.

'With . . . whatever it is you're
trying to get away with!' I said,
realising I still wasn't sure exactly
what the man was up to with his
creepy weedy-army. But I was
fully expecting a big long rant
about taking over the world
– that's what criminal
                        masterminds
                        and evil
                        geniuses
                        always do.

'You're too late, little girl!' the thin man said. 'My troops are ready! Once dispatched they will creep into every garden and spread into every field and farm in the world . . .'

If evil geniuses and criminal masterminds didn't spend so much time ranting about their plans to take over the world, they'd probably be a lot more successful. But they love bragging about how clever they are – so I used the time to look for a way to stop him. My eyes fell on my shopping trolley sitting in the aisle behind him.

'. . . my weed army will control every crop on the planet!' he continued. 'Then I will hold the whole world to ransom!' With one careful flick of my grabber-hand I extended it behind the man and into the trolley. Then, grabbing a big terracotta pot, I flicked it up in the air and dropped it on his head.

'OW!' The man growled,
rubbing the top of his head angrily.

It didn't knock him out but he
was distracted long enough for me to
shoot past.

I grabbed the handle of the
trolley and ran as fast as I could.
The trolley had
filled up quite a
bit while I was
pretending
to be a
shopper,
so it
quickly
picked
up
speed. Once it
was going fast enough I leapt into the

basket and rode it through the aisles
of greenhouses.

Looking back, I saw the man
stoop down to whisper to the weed
army gathered at his feet, then he
nodded in my direction and the
weeds suddenly started chasing me!

They shot across the floor
hissing and waving their
leaves.

Rummaging
inside the trolley
for stuff to
throw
at them
I laid my
hands on two
green

spray bottles. I lifted them out and
was about to lob them at the gaining
vegetation when I caught sight of the
labels.

SUPER STRONG WEED KILLER!

Squirt!

Squir

I quickly
flicked the caps
off the bottles with my
thumbs, curled my fingers
round the plastic triggers and as the
first of the weeds leapt into the air I
squirted them!

They instantly fell away,
landing with a splat, but the others
kept on coming.

Squirt! Squirt! Squirt!

As the last angry weed splatted
on the floor in a limp mushy heap,

Squirt!

Squirt!

I looked back at the thin man.
Needless to say, he'd lost his I'm-
going-to-rule-the-world smile. It
was now replaced with the equally
familiar my-life's-work-is-ruined
grimace!

He wouldn't be causing any trouble in a hurry!

I was about to feel pleased with myself for saving the world again, when I suddenly realised I was still sitting in a trolley moving at very high speed through aisles of greenhouses.

Uh Oh!

I leapt off the trolley and grabbed the handle. Digging my heels into the floor, again I managed to steer to avoid one crash, only to send the trolley hurtling round the corner and into the main section of the garden centre!

Still
holding on,
the trolley dragged
me through the leafy aisles
when suddenly I heard a thud and a
very startled 'yelp'!

I peered over the top of the handle and saw a very dazed Trudy sitting in the trolley with her arms and legs hanging over the sides. Picking up an unexpected passenger definitely slowed the trolley down but peering through Trudy's legs I saw something up ahead – something we were heading straight for.

It was the check out till, and standing beside it was Mum and Trudy's dad.

They both looked up at the same time and their mouths fell open.

CRASH! OOPS!

On the way home in the car Mum was silent. She usually gives me the 'silent treatment' when she's really angry. It happens quite a lot because saving the world often gets me into trouble.

In fact, Mum only spoke once during the whole trip home.

'That girl Trudy is clearly a very bad influence on you and I don't want to see you hanging around with her again,' Mum growled, shaking her head at the memory of Trudy and me crashing into the check out till and overturning the trolley.

'OK,' I said, thinking this was a bit of a bonus.

'And on second thoughts,' Mum added, glancing back at my bulging rucksack, 'perhaps you *are* better off playing with your dolls, they're definitely a lot less dangerous!'

Watch out for my second book

AGENT Amelia Zombie Cows!

Three more fabulously funny stories!

COMING SOON!

He disappeared from the window...a door slammed inside the house, a trampling on the stairs...he burst out the kitchen door...a flying leap off the back steps. He rolled, scrambled up, yelling, "I win! I win! I win!" Grabbed Tom's hands. They danced round and round and round, Pete cavorting beside them.

Joe and Alan slunk off through the bushes.

...Round and round and round...

Billy's mother laughed and went into the kitchen.

...Round and round and round...till they collapsed on their backs in the grass.

"I win," gasped Billy to the blue, cloudless sky. "I win."

EPILOGUE

Billy leaned the minibike against a tree and started down the path through the woods. Tom and Joe were already sitting by a smouldering trash fire on the riverbank, opening their lunch bags.

"Where's Alan? At the shops?" asked Billy, flopping down by Tom.

"Yeah," said Joe. "He's still got two weeks to go."

"What have you got for lunch?" asked Tom.

Billy looked embarrassed.

"Worm-and-egg on rye."

"Heck," said Tom. "Why can't you ever bring something somebody else likes, so you can trade?"

Billy frowned. He opened his lunch bag.

"I don't know. I just can't stop. I don't dare tell my mother. I even like the taste now." He scratched his head. "Do you think there's something the doctors don't know? Do you think I could be the first person who's ever been hooked on worms?"

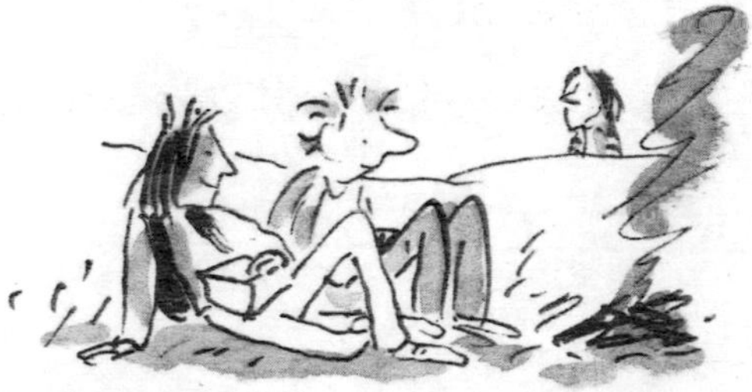

IF YOU LIKE HOW TO EAT FRIED WORMS, YOU'LL LOVE

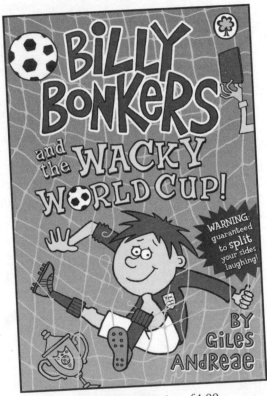

978 1 40833 058 6   £4.99

ORCHARD

Steel Lecture for

Time, wrote the b

eekly column for the *Guardian* and now does so fo

Independent. He lives in London.

Reasons to be Cheerful

From Punk to New Labour through the Eyes of a Dedicated Troublemaker

Mark Steel

Scribner

First published in Great Britain by Scribner, 2001
This edition published by Scribner, 2002
An imprint of Simon & Schuster UK Ltd
A Viacom Company

Scribner and design are trademarks of Macmillan Library Reference USA, Inc.,
used under license by Simon & Schuster, the publisher of this work.

1 3 5 7 9 10 8 6 4 2

Simon & Schuster UK Ltd
Africa House
64–78 Kingsway
London WC2B 6AH

Simon & Schuster Australia
Sydney

A CIP catalogue record for this book is available from the British Library

ISBN 0-7432-0804-8

Typeset in Sabon by SX Composing DTP, Rayleigh, Essex
Printed and bound in Great Britain by Clays Ltd, St Ives plc

Acknowledgements

I would like to thank Mac McKenna and Pat Stack, with whom I spent many joyful hours discussing the various periods I was writing about, though often we'd end up in a stupor from which none of us can remember what was said. Martin Valentine provided a similar service and, crucially, a room in which to write the thing. Jonny Geller was astute enough to tell me what was wrong with my first draft. So however shit you consider this is, if it wasn't for him it would be worse. My partner Bindy deserves many thanks. And my son Elliot deserves boundless praise for not once doing what would have been a classic three-year-old nugget of behaviour, and calmly pressing 'delete' to whisk days of labour into the parallel universe occupied by lost words from computers.

Lastly I must thank Tony Cliff (1917–2000), without whom this book, and so much else, would not have been possible. Including the survival into the twenty-first century of the following joke, which he told so often, as a reminder that all we are up against is what's in our own heads.

An Arab businessman comes to Britain to buy a cooling system for his palace. So he visits a factory where they're made, and the managing director tries to sell him one, but the Arab is distracted because at twelve o'clock the hooter goes. He watches everyone leave and nudges the manager. 'Look, look,' he panics, 'your slaves are all leaving.' 'Don't worry, they'll be back,' says the manager. The Arab is so stunned he can't concentrate, but at one o'clock the hooter goes and, as predicted, everyone comes back. At the end of the day the manager says to the Arab, 'Well, would you like to buy a cooling system?' And the Arab says, 'Sod the cooling system, get me ten of them hooters.'

Introduction

The people I find most infuriating are the perenially miserable: the sort who say 'just my luck' or 'story of my life, that is'. I feel like saying to them, 'Look. If you are a Hutu from Rwanda who accidentally strolls into an armed Tutsi warrior camp, then you are entitled to go "Huh, just my luck. Story of my life." But if you've gone down the shops for a packet of biscuits and they've run out of your favourite sort, shut the fuck up and put up with it.'

For much of the last twenty-five years, some of the most disconsolate people have been found amongst the section of society that wishes the world to be more equal, more, shall we say, socialist. Thatcher, then Blair and their big business chums can appear to have had everything their own way. Worse, in Britain people are often told to 'stop talking about politics, it only causes arguments'. But you can only have that attitude if politics doesn't appear to affect your life. If the house was burning down, and one group was urging everyone to 'run through the flames' while someone else shouted that the only chance was to jump, even my Mum wouldn't say 'Stop talking about fires, it will only cause a row. Now let's have a nice cup of tea and burn to death.'

Away from the sleepiness of Westminster, the period covered in this book has presented many reasons to be cheerful. Because politics is about more than ministers and by-elections, treasury statements and passionless automatons reciting their dry, wizened statements on *Newsnight*. So, although this book is about politics, it isn't about 'politics' or politicians. And although it's a personal account, it isn't about me. Instead, this is a story of the frustrations and exhilaration of the twists and turns, the slow drips and sudden explosions that have affected all of us over those twenty-five years. It's the story of momentous events seen through the eyes of one individual playing a small part in those events.

For nothing ever stays the same. Even since finishing this book there has been revolution in Serbia, and an enthusiastic, largely nose-studded movement has developed around the world to confront bodies such as the World Bank and the International Monetary Fund. Maybe, by the time this is published, Tony Blair and his free market chums will have been swept away, rendering this entire book out-of-date. Wouldn't that be just my luck, the story of my life?

Chapter 1

I'll start with the happy ending; I don't like Tony Blair or New Labour. I've never liked them and I knew all along I didn't like them.

This is the optimistic outcome of the twenty-five years covered in this book. Not that many other people like them, though lots thought they did, because they didn't feel anything better was possible. So polls showed Blair as the most popular Prime Minister of the 20th century. But who do you know who liked him? No one. He was the most unpopular most popular person there had ever been. He reminded me of an irritating idiot at a party, who everyone wishes would leave, but no one dares tell him to because everyone thinks he's everyone else's friend.

Being aware of not liking him is the culmination of a journey which, to begin with, I didn't know I was on. Adopted children sometimes go to great lengths to discover their natural parents, feeling it would explain how they are what they are. But few of us consider the events and trends, booms, crises and political upheavals that swirl around us, whisking us through the markers of our lives.

In fact we are prisoners of our times. We can live by the philosophy that if we show initiative, we'll be rewarded with promotion and wealth, but only because we no longer live in a feudal system in which power is inherited. No peasant in the 12th century believed that if he worked extra hours each day on Lord Hertfordshire's estate, he might end up as his son, and inherit Hemel Hempstead. Someone might be a vegetarian, but had they been around 500 years ago, they would have skinned rabbits joyfully, and if they'd found a tofu-based sausage, grassed up the owner as a witch. And a person may identify themselves as proud to be a Londoner, and a supporter of West Ham. But had they been taken from birth and brought up in the Amazon, they wouldn't have grown up flogging second-hand canoes, and yelling 'You're shit and you know you are,' at a family of baboons.

The first influence on my political direction was to be brought up in Swanley, on the border between outer London and Kent. Most people brought up in small towns complain about the lack of entertainment, and the soporific atmosphere, and many insist that their particular example is worse than any other. But telling someone from Swanley about the tedium of your small town, is like saying to Nelson Mandela, 'I've had hassle from the old bill myself, so I know how you feel mate.'

There was no cinema, no venue for bands, no theatre, and in a town two miles long, about one and a half miles wide and consisting of 25,000 people, there were three pubs and a Chinese take-away. There was a small sports centre, which almost everyone went to, but what difference did this make? When you're a sixteen-year-old boy, if a girl agrees to go out with you, you can't say, 'Great. Let's go weight-training.'

But the lack of facilities was only part of the problem. Swanley was built around domesticity. Its population had quadrupled in ten years, not because it offered work, but because it offered housing, out of the hubbub of London. So its *purpose* was boredom. The stultifying listlessness of the place seeped through the emptiness of the new estates and the deserted main road, which pottered past a fenced-off stagnant pond, Woolworths, and away up to the big city that was Sidcup. Swanley was *never* busy. If you were out after eight o'clock, you'd see only the odd lonesome individual walking their dog, and a feel a camaraderie, the way you might if you met someone up a mountain on Christmas Day.

Boredom is a state of mind, rather than a lack of things to do. So the honourable attempts to combat the lethargy by setting up a pottery class or amateur dramatics group didn't affect the overall atmosphere. There were no collective activities, not even a regular market place. There was no cultural mix, not even a curry house.

When I was fifteen, a group of us would meet in the evenings and play records. Occasionally, for a change, we'd wander the streets. We'd drink a tin of beer between us, pull up someone's flowers, and one night we smashed every pane of glass in some poor sod's greenhouse.

Maybe it's no coincidence that so many revolutionaries come from small towns. Marx was from Triere, Robespierre from Arras, his protégé St Just from Picardy, Lenin from Simbirsk, and Trotsky from the Ukrainian town of Bobrinetz. When Trotsky was 15, I wonder if he spent evenings hanging around a Bobrinetz bus shelter, destroying a peasant's allotment while sipping a third of a tin of Heineken, and thinking, 'There's got to be more to life than this.'

The philosophy of my generation was shaped in part by the notion universally held during our childhood, that as time went on the population would become wealthier. From the war onwards, the economy had been booming, and every year brought a life-changing new gadget; fridge, washing machine, TV, vacuum cleaner or car. Your kids would have an easier life than you, jammy sods, with 'all the opportunities we never had'.

Everyone at that time believed that, within reason, you could choose the job you wanted, and follow it for the rest of your life. 'What are you going to be when you grow up?' adults would ask with annoying regularity. If you didn't know, you'd get a follow-up statement that went, 'Take my advice son, get a trade.' Followed by that wink which that generation did when talking to ten-year-olds. But it's a question you just don't hear any more. It would sound as archaic as 'forsooth sire', or 'two-bob bit'.

The worst that could happen would be to end up in an unskilled job.

'I know where you'll end up,' a chemistry teacher screamed at me when he caught me skipping a lesson, 'You'll end up DRIVING A VAN.' These days they must sit down with the bright kid of the class, and say, 'If you continue with this high standard of work, study hard, get your GCSEs, go to university and come out with a good degree, with a bit of luck you could end up driving a van.'

My parents' generation had been promised security and gradual material improvements. If they worked hard and saved a bit each year they could end up in a nice house, full of china ornaments, that their parents could only have dreamed of. And for many the promise appeared to have been kept.

My dad was the son of a bus driver, spent the war in the navy, and worked in an engineering factory through the fifties, until he became the local insurance man. On an average wage, he bought a garden with a bungalow front and back. He could believe that hi-fi stereos and James Last box sets came to those who grafted. As a result, my dad bought things, like a commemorative plate wrapped in crinkly paper inside a furry box to mark cricketer Colin Cowdrey's hundredth hundred – because 'that'll be worth a few bob one day, son' (wink).

Almost every line of thought from that generation led to money. The response to any career mentioned was either 'good money in that' or 'not much money in that'. If someone bought you anything that looked slightly classy, like a wooden model aeroplane, they would say 'look after that, and one day it could be worth a lot of money'. I wonder if any of us ever took them up on this advice, and at the age of thirty visited Sotheby's, smugly inquiring, 'How much can I expect for this little beauty?', presenting a nine-inch brass tram from the Isle of Man.

My mum worked sometimes, part-time, though it didn't seem to matter much if she didn't. 'I'm going out to get a job,' she said, and walked fifty yards to the electric organ factory, where she was told she could start the next day, in the manner of new characters in *Coronation St* wandering into the Rovers to get taken on by Mike Baldwin. But there was one enormous exception to the notion that material possessions were a reward for graft: *them*.

Sociologists and economists concoct elaborate categories to describe classes in society, but to most of that generation, there was only one class apart from their own; *them*. If my parents had devised these socio-economic groupings, the top category wouldn't have been 'managerial and executive', or 'A and B1' but 'la-di-da types'. Them who didn't appreciate money because they'd always had it. Them who have prawn cocktails and wine so often they've forgotten it's a treat. Them who watch BBC2.

As an engineer my dad must have been a member of the strong post-war unions, which secured rapidly improving pay and conditions. And there lies the contradiction of that generation. They believed their share of the stability, and holidays in the Isle of Wight, bungalows, a health service and vacancies at the organ